STEPHEN LEACOCK'S SELF-MADE MEN

SIX HUMORUS ESSAYS

ADAPTED BY:
JEROME TILLER
ILLUSTRATED BY:
MARC JOHNSON-PENCOOK

Adapted Classics for Middle School
An imprint of ArtWrite Productions
1555 Gardena Ave NE
Minneapolis, MN 55432-5848

Book Design by ArtWrite Productions
Cover Design by Kristina Brown

ISBN 978-1-939846-33-4

adaptedclassics.com

kristinadesignz.com

artwriteproductions.com

PREFACE

You are about to read adapted versions of six essays by Stephen Leacock, a world-renowned author and humorist. Some changes (paragraph breaks, rearrangements, minor additions and omissions, etc.) were made to accommodate the illustration of characters and critical scenes in the essays. Some changes (word choice, word order, minor additions, etc.) were made to expand its accessibility and appeal, keeping modern youth in mind. No change was made with the notion it would improve the text or the essay.

Among other places, the original version of each essay can be found at: http://www.gutenberg.org/

CONTENTS

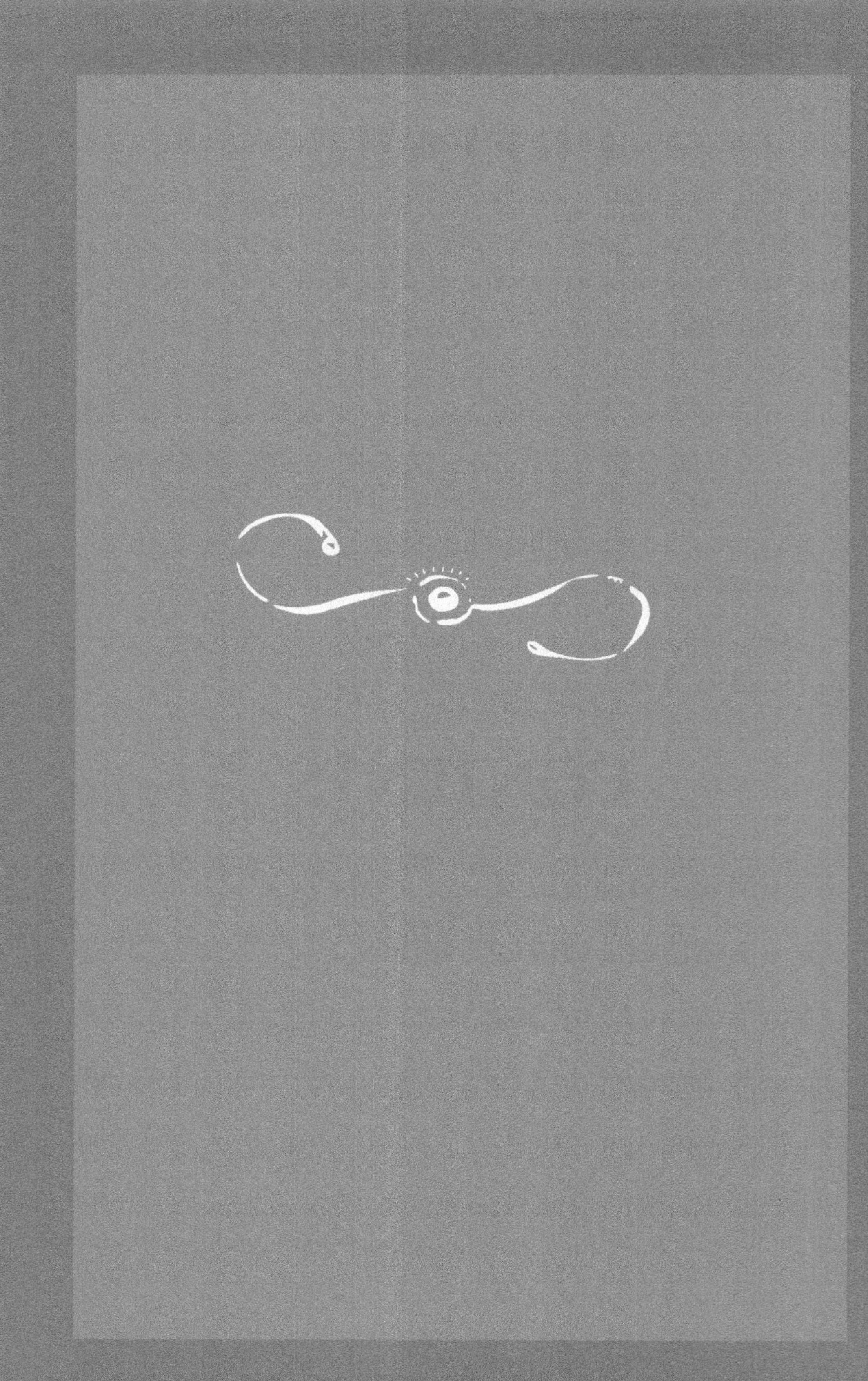

SELF-MADE MEN

They were both what we commonly call successful business men—men with well-fed faces, heavy signet rings on fingers like sausages, and broad, comfortable waistcoats, a yard and a half round the equator. They were seated opposite each other at a table of a first-class restaurant, and had fallen into conversation while waiting to give their order to the waiter. Their talk had drifted back to their early days and how each had made his start in life when he first struck New York.

"I tell you what, Jones," one of them was saying, "I shall never forget my first few years in this town. By George, it was pretty uphill work! Do you know, sir, when I first struck this place, I hadn't more than fifteen cents to my name, hadn't a rag except what I stood up in, and all the place I had to sleep in—you won't believe it, but it's a gospel fact just the same—was an empty tar barrel. No, sir," he went on, leaning back and closing up his eyes into an expression of infinite experience, "no, sir, a fellow accustomed to luxury like you has simply no idea what sleeping out in a tar barrel and all that kind of thing is like."

"My dear Robinson," the other man rejoined briskly, "if you imagine I've had no experience of hardship of that sort, you never made a bigger mistake in your life. Why, when I first walked into this town I hadn't a cent, sir, not a cent, and as for lodging, all the place I had for months and months was an old piano box up a lane, behind a factory. Talk about hardship, I guess I had it pretty rough! You take a fellow that's used to a good warm tar barrel and put him into a piano box for a night or two, and you'll see mighty soon—"

"My dear fellow," Robinson broke in with some irritation, "you merely show that you don't know what a tar barrel's like. Why, on winter nights, when you'd be shut in there in your piano box just as snug as you please, I used to lie awake shivering, with the draft fairly running in at the bunghole at the back."

"Draft!" sneered the other man, with a provoking laugh, "Draft! Don't talk to me about drafts. This box I speak of had a whole darned plank off it, right on the north side too. I used to sit there studying in the evenings, and the snow would blow in a foot deep. And yet, sir," he continued more quietly, "though I know you'll not believe it, I don't mind admitting that some of the happiest days of my life were spent in that same old box. Ah, those were good old times! Bright, innocent days, I can tell you. I'd wake up there in the mornings and fairly shout with high spirits. Of course, you may not be able to stand that kind of life—"

"Not stand it!" cried Robinson fiercely; "me not stand it! By gad! I'm made for it. I just wish I had a taste of the old life again for a while. And as for innocence! Well, I'll bet you weren't one-tenth as innocent as I was; no, nor one-fifth, nor one-third! What a grand old life it was! You'll swear this is a darned lie and refuse to believe it—but I can remember evenings when I'd have two or three fellows in, and we'd sit round and play go fish by a candle half the night."

"Two or three!" laughed Jones; "why, my dear fellow, I've known half a dozen of us to sit down to supper in my piano box, and have a game of go fish afterwards; yes, and charades and forfeits, and every other darned thing. Mighty good suppers they were too! By Jove, Robinson, you fellows round this town who have ruined your digestions with high living, have no notion of the zest with which a man can sit down to a few potato peelings, or a bit of broken pie crust, or—"

Talk about hard food," interrupted the other, "I guess I know all about that. Many's the time I've breakfasted off a little cold porridge that somebody was going to throw away from a back-door, or that I've gone round to a livery stable and begged a little bran mash that they intended for the pigs. I'll venture to say I've eaten more hog's food—"

"Hog's food!" shouted Robinson, striking his fist savagely on the table, "I tell you hog's food suits me better than—"

He stopped speaking with a sudden grunt of surprise as the waiter appeared with the question:

"What may I bring you for dinner, gentlemen?"

"Dinner!" said Jones, after a moment of silence. "Dinner! Oh, anything, nothing—I never care what I eat—give me a little cold porridge, if you've got it, or a chunk of salt pork—anything you like, it's all the same to me."

The waiter turned with an impassive face to Robinson.

"You can bring me some of that cold porridge too," he said, with a defiant look at Jones; "yesterday's, if you have it, and a few potato peelings and a glass of skim milk."

There was a pause. Jones sat back in his chair and looked hard across at Robinson. For some moments the two men gazed into each other's eyes with a stern, defiant intensity. Then Robinson turned slowly round in his seat and beckoned to the waiter, who was moving off with the muttered order on his lips.

"Here, waiter," he said with a savage scowl, "I guess I'll change that order a little. Instead of that cold porridge I'll take—um, yes—a little hot partridge. And you might as well bring me an oyster or two on the half shell, and a mouthful of soup (mock-turtle, consomme, anything), and perhaps you might fetch along a dab of fish, and a little peck of Stilton cheese, and a grape, or a walnut."

The waiter turned to Jones.

"I guess I'll take the same," he said simply, and added; "and you might bring a quart of champagne at the same time."

And nowadays, when Jones and Robinson meet, the memory of the tar barrel and the piano box is buried as far out of sight as a home for the blind under a landslide.

HOW TO MAKE A MILLION DOLLARS

I mix a good deal with the Millionaires. I like them. I like their faces. I like the way they live. I like the things they eat. The more we mix together the better I like the things we mix.

Especially I like the way they dress, their grey check trousers, their white check waist-coats, their heavy gold chains, and the signet-rings they sign their checks with. My, they look nice! Get six or seven of them sitting together in the club and it's a treat to see them. And if they get the least dust on them, men come and brush it off. Yes, and are glad to. I'd like to take some of the dust off them myself.

Even more than what they eat I like their intellectual grasp. It is wonderful. Just watch them read. Their brains never tire. They simply read all the time. Go into the club at any hour and you'll see three or four of them at it. And the things they can read! You'd think that a man who'd been driving hard in the office from eleven o'clock until three, with only an hour and a half for lunch, would be too fagged. Not a bit. These men can sit down after office hours and read the The National Enquirer, the Police Gazette, Star, People, and the Wrestling Weekly and dive into the depths of them just as well as I can.

What I love to do is to walk up and down among them and catch the little scraps of conversation. The other day I heard one lean forward and say, "Well, I offered him a million and a half and said I wouldn't give a cent more, he could either take it or leave it—"

I just longed to break in and say, "What! What! A million and a half! Oh, say that again! Offer it to me, to either take it or leave it. Do try me once: I know I can: or here, make it a plain million and let's call it done."

Not that these men are careless over money. No, sir. Don't think it. Of course they don't take much account of big money, a hundred thousand dollars at a shot or anything of that sort. But little money? You've no idea till you know them how anxious they get about a quarter, or dime, or less.

Why, two of them came into the club the other night just frantic with delight: they said wheat had risen and they'd cleaned up ten bucks each in less than half an hour. They both bought a dinner for ninety-six bucks on the strength of it. I don't understand it. I've often made twice as much as ten bucks waiting tables but I didn't feel much like boasting about it.

One night I heard one man say, "Well, let's call up New York and offer them a slice of the pie". Great heavens! Imagine paying the cost of calling up New York, nearly eleven million people, late at night and offering them a slice of their pie! And yet—did New York get mad? No, they took it. Of course it's high finance. I don't pretend to understand it. I tried after that to call up Chicago and offer it a pie and a half, and to call up Hamilton, Ontario, and offer it half a dozen cookies, and the phone operators only thought I was crazy.

All this shows, of course, that I've been studying how the millionaires do it. I have. For years. I thought it might be helpful to young men just beginning to work and anxious to stop.

You know, many a man realizes late in life that had he known what he knows now, then instead of being what he is, he might have been what he isn't. But how few boys stop to think that if they only knew now what they don't know, then instead of being what they will be, they'd be what they won't be? These are awful thoughts.

At any rate, I've been gathering hints on how it is they do it. One thing I'm sure about. If a young man wants to make a million dollars he's got to be mighty careful about his diet and his living. This may seem hard. But success is only achieved with pains.

There is no use in a young man who hopes to make a million dollars thinking he's entitled to get up at 7:30, eat flat bread and poached eggs, drink cold water at lunch, and go to bed at 10 p.m. You can't do it. I've seen too many millionaires for that. If you want to be a millionaire you mustn't get up till ten in the morning. They never do. They dare not. It would fiddle away as much as their business is worth if they were seen on the street at half-past nine.

And the old idea of temperance is all wrong. To be a millionaire you need champagne, lots of it, and all the time. That, and Scotch whiskey and soda. You have to sit up nearly all night and drink buckets of it. This is what clears the brain for business the next day. I've seen some of these men with their brains so clear in the morning that their faces look positively boiled.

To live like this requires, of course, resolution. But you can get that from any one of the dozens of self-help books on the shelves at your local library.

Therefore, my dear young man, if you want to get moved on from your present status in business, change your life. When your landlady brings you oatmeal with unbuttered toast for breakfast, throw them out the window for whatever dog might eat that kind of stuff and tell her to bring you some well-marbled steak, slathered with garlic, onions, and cheese, and a serving bowl of spiked party punch to wash it down. Then telephone your employer and say that you'll be down about eleven o'clock. You will get moved on from your present staus. Yes, very quickly.

Just how the millionaires make the money is a difficult question. But one way is this. Strike the town with twenty-five cents in your pocket. They nearly all do this. they've told me again and again (men with millions and millions) that the first time they struck town they had only twenty-five cents. That seems to have given them their start.

Of course, it's not easy to do. I've tried it several times. I nearly did it once. I borrowed twenty-five cents, carried it away out of town, and then turned and came back at the town in an awful rush. If I hadn't passed a carnival in the suburbs and spent the twenty-five cents, I might have been rich today.

Another good plan is to start something. Something on a huge scale—something nobody ever thought of. For instance, one man I know told me that once he was down in Mexico without a cent (he'd lost his twenty-five just before striking the border) and he noticed that they had no power plants. So he started some and made a mint of money. Another man that I know was once stranded in New York, absolutely without a nickel. Well, it occurred to him that what was needed were buildings ten stories higher than any that had been put up. So he built two and sold them right away. Ever so many millionaires begin in some such simple way as that.

There is, of course, a much easier way than any of these. I almost hate to tell this, because I want to do it myself.

I learned of it just by chance one night at the club. There is one old man there, extremely rich, with one of the best faces of the lot, just like a hyena. I never used to know how he had got so rich. So one evening I asked one of the millionaires how old Bloggs had made all his money.

"How he made it?" he answered with a sneer. "Why he made it by taking it out of widows and orphans."

Widows and orphans! I thought, what an excellent idea. But who would have suspected that they had it?

"And how," I asked pretty cautiously, "did he go at it to get it out of them?"

"Why," the man answered, "he just ground them under his heels, that was how."

Now isn't that simple? I've thought of that conversation often since and I mean to try it. If I can get hold of them, I'll grind them quick enough. But how to get them. Most of the widows I know look pretty solid for that sort of thing, and as for orphans, it must take an awful lot of them. Meantime I am waiting, and if I ever get a large bunch of orphans all together, I'll stamp on them and see.

I find, too, on inquiry, that you also can grind it out of most clergymen of any type. They say they grind nicely. But perhaps orphans are easier.

HOW TO LIVE TO BE 200

Twenty years ago I knew a man called Jiggins who had the Health Habit. He used to take a cold plunge every morning. He said it opened his pores. After that he did a hot sponge. He said it closed the pores. He got so that he could open and shut his pores at will.

Jiggins used to stand and breathe at an open window for half an hour before dressing. He said it expanded his lungs. He might, of course, have done as much for them had he vented vigorously each morning at his new neighbor whose barking dogs were robbing him of sleep. But after all, he risks no loss of teeth, blood, or self-respect this way, and who wants to confront a six-foot-nine owner of Rottweilers anyway?

After he had got his undershirt on, Jiggins used to hitch himself up like a dog in harness and do dumbbell exercises. He did them forwards, backwards, and hind-side up. He could have got a job being a dog anywhere.

He spent all his time at this kind of thing. In his spare time at the office, he used to lie on his stomach on the floor and see if he could lift himself up with his knuckles. If he could, then he tried some other way until he found one that he couldn't do. Then he would spend the rest of his spare time and his entire lunch hour on his stomach, perfectly happy.

In the evenings in his room he used to lift iron bars, cannon balls, heave dumbbells, and haul himself up to the ceiling with his teeth. You could hear the thumps half a mile away. He liked it.

He spent half the night slinging himself around his room. He said it made his brain clear. When he got his brain perfectly clear, he went to bed and slept. As soon as he woke, he began clearing it again.

Jiggins is dead. He was, of course, a pioneer, but the fact that he dumbbelled himself to death at an early age does not prevent a whole generation of young men from following in his path, ridden by the Health Mania.

They make themselves a nuisance. They get up at impossible hours. They go out in silly little suits and run Marathon heats before breakfast. They chase around barefoot to get the dew on their feet. They hunt for ozone.

They bother about pepsin. They won't eat meat because it has too much nitrogen. They won't eat fruit because it hasn't any. They prefer albumen and starch and nitrogen to huckleberry pie and doughnuts.

They won't drink water out of a tap. They won't eat sardines out of a can. They won't use oysters out of a pail. They won't drink milk out of a glass. They are afraid of alcohol in any shape, even the wine at church on Sundays. Yes, sir, afraid. And after all their fuss they presently incur some simple old-fashioned illness and die like anybody else. God rest their souls.

Now people of this sort have no chance to attain a wonderously fulfilling old life before their hereafters. They are on the wrong track. Do you really want to live to get way, way old, enjoy a grand, green, exuberant, boastful old age, and then make yourself a nuisance to your whole neighborhood with your reminiscences? Come on, now!

So if not, then cut out all this nonsense. Cut it out. Get up in the morning at a sensible hour. The time to get up is when you have to, not before. If your office opens at eleven, get up at ten-thirty. Take your chance on ozone. There isn't any such thing anyway. Or, if there is, you can buy a Thermos bottle full for five cents, and put it on a shelf in your cupboard.

If your work begins at seven in the morning, get up at ten minutes to, but don't be liar enough to say that you like it. It isn't exhilarating, and you know it.

Also, drop all that cold-bath business. You never did it when you were a boy. Don't be a fool now.

If you must take a bath (you don't really need to), take it warm. The pleasure of getting out of a cold bed and creeping into a hot bath beats a cold plunge to death. In any case, stop gassing about your tub and your "shower," as if you were the only man who ever washed. So much for that point.

Next, take the question of germs and bacilli. Don't be scared of them. That's all. That's the whole thing. And if you once get on to that you never need to worry again.

If you see a bacilli, walk right up to it, and look it in the eye. If one flies into your room, strike at it with your hat or with a towel. Hit it as hard as you can between the neck and the thorax. It will soon get sick of that.

But as a matter of fact, a bacilli is perfectly quiet and harmless if you are not afraid of it. Speak to it. Call out to it to "lie down." It will understand.

I had a bacilli once, called Fido, that would come and lie at my feet while I was working. I never knew a more affectionate companion, and when it was run over by an automobile, I buried it in the garden with genuine sorrow. (I admit this is an exaggeration. I don't really remember its name—it may have been Robert.)

Understand that it is only a fad of modern medicine to say that cholera and typhoid and diphtheria are caused by bacilli and germs. Nonsense! Cholera is caused by a frightful pain in the stomach, and diphtheria is caused by trying to cure a sore throat.

Now take the question of food. Eat what you want. Eat lots of it. Yes, eat too much of it. Eat everything that you like until you can't eat any more. Eat till you can just stagger across the room with it barely secured within, prop yourself up against a sofa cushion, and relax and enjoy. The only test is, can you pay for it? If you can't pay for it, don't eat it.

And listen—don't worry as to whether your food contains starch, or albumen, or gluten, or nitrogen. If you are damn fool enough to want these things, go and buy them and eat all you want of them. Go to a laundry and get a bag of starch and eat your fill of it. Eat it, and take a good long drink of glue after it, and a spoonful of Portland cement. That will gluten you, good and solid.

If you like nitrogen, go and get a druggist to give you a can full of it at the soda counter and let you sip it with a straw. Only don't think that you can mix all these things up with your food. There isn't any nitrogen or phosphorus or albumen in ordinary things to eat. In any decent household all that sort of stuff is washed out in the kitchen sink before the food is put on the table.

And just one word about fresh air. Don't bother with it. Get your room full of good air, then shut up the windows and keep it. It will keep for years. And don't keep using your lungs all the time. Let them rest.

As for exercise, if you have to take it, take it and put up with it. But as long as you have the price of a cab and can pay to watch other people play baseball, or can watch others run races or others do gymnastics while you sit in the shade and smoke and watch them—great heavens, what more do you want?

HOW TO SUCCEED IN LIFE

Let me begin with a sort of parable. Many years ago when I was on the staff of a great public school, we engaged a new swimming master. He was the most successful man in that capacity that we had had for years.

Then one day it was discovered that he couldn't swim. He was standing at the edge of the swimming tank explaining the breast stroke to the boys in the water. He lost his balance and fell in. He was drowned. Or no, he wasn't drowned, at least not for once and for all—he was rescued by some of the pupils whom he had taught to swim.

After he was resuscitated by the boys—it was one of the things he had taught them—the school dismissed him.

Then some of the boys who were sorry for him taught him how to swim, and he got a new job as a swimming master in another place. But this time he was an utter failure. He swam well, but they said he couldn't teach.

So his friends looked about to get him a new job. This was just at the time when the bicycle craze came in. They soon found the man a position as an instructor in bicycle riding. As he had never been on a bicycle in his life, he made an admirable teacher. He stood fast on the ground and said, "Now then, all you need is confidence."

Then one day he got afraid that he might be found out. So he went out to a quiet place and got on a bicycle, at the top of a slope, to learn to ride it. The bicycle ran away with him. But for the skill and daring of one of his pupils, who saw him and rode after him, he would have been killed.

This story, as the reader sees, is endless. Suffice it to say that the man I speak of is now in an aviation school teaching people to fly. They say he is one of the best aviators that ever walked.

According to all the legends and story books, the principal factor in success is perseverance. Personally, I think there is nothing in it. There is an old motto that runs, "If at first you don't succeed, try, try again." This is nonsense. If anything, the truth lies the other way. It ought to read, "If at first you don't succeed, quit, quit, at once." If you can't do a thing, more or less, the first time you try, you will never do it. Try something else while there is yet time.

Let me illustrate this with a story. I remember, long years ago, at a little school that I attended in the country, we had a schoolmaster, who used perpetually to write on the blackboard, in a fine hand, the motto that I have just quoted:

> "If at first you don't succeed,
> Try, try, again."

He wore plain clothes and had a hard, determined face. He was studying for some sort of preliminary medical examination, and was saving money for a medical course. Every now and then he went away to the city and tried the examination: and he always failed. Each time he came back, he would write up on the blackboard:

> "Try, try again."

And always he looked grimmer and more determined than before. The strange thing was that, with all his industry and determination, he would break out every now and then, lie down in a crossroad, enter into deep meditation, and the school would be shut for two days. Then he came back, more fiercely resolute than ever. Even children could see that the man's life was a fight to the end.

Well, after he had tried it four times, the schoolmaster at last passed the examination. He went away to the city in a suit of store clothes, with eight hundred dollars that he had saved up, to study medicine. Now it happened that he had a brother who was not a bit like himself, but was a sort of ne'er-do-well, always hard-up and sponging on other people, and never working.

And when the schoolmaster came to the city and his brother knew that he had eight hundred dollars, he came to him, took him aside, and persuaded him to hand it over— all eight hundred dollars—to put it into the Louisiana State lottery. In those days you could buy a ticket for one dollar. The Grand Prize was two hundred thousand dollars, and the two runner-ups were a hundred thousand each.

So the brother persuaded the schoolmaster to put the money in. He said he had a system for buying only the tickets with prime numbers, that won't divide by anything, and that it must win. He said it was a mathematical certainty. He showed the plan of it to the schoolmaster on a table in the dining hall of a church using a stack of bingo cards and a box of dominoes. He told the schoolmaster that he himself would only take ten per cent of what they made, as a commission for showing the system, and the schoolmaster could have the rest. So, in a mad moment, the schoolmaster handed over his roll of money, and that was the last he ever saw of it.

The next morning when he was up, he was full of remorse for what he had done. He could not go back to the school, and he had no money to go forward. So he stayed where he was in the little hotel where he began to fast, pray, and meditate again. Before long he became so emaciated and unkempt that the hotel staff were afraid for him. They watched him out of the corners of their eyes wondering what he would do when he occasionally appeared, mumbling prayers and stumbling as if in a trance.

But they knew that there was only one end possible, and they waited for it to come, and presently it did. One of the porters went up to the schoolmaster's room to bring up a letter, and he found him lying on the bed with his face gray as ashes, and his eyes looking up at the ceiling. He was stone dead. Life had beaten him.

And the strange thing was that the letter that the porter carried up that morning was from the management of the Louisiana Lottery. It contained a draft on New York, signed by the treasurer of the State of Louisiana, for two hundred thousand dollars. The schoolmaster had won the Grand Prize.

The above story, I am afraid, is a little gloomy. I am putting it down merely for the moral it contains. But now I have become so absorbed in telling it that I forget what the moral was that it was meant to convey. Was it that if you are committed to praying to God for a favor, at least eat something while you are waiting for an answer?

No, I think the idea is that if the schoolmaster had long before abandoned the study of medicine, for which he was not fitted, and gone in, let us say, for playing the banjo, he might have become a rhythm master in a minstrel show. Yes, that's it.

Let me pass on to other elements in success. I suppose that anybody will admit that the peculiar quality that is called initiative—the ability to act promptly on one's own judgment—is a factor of the highest importance. I have seen this illustrated two or three times in a very striking fashion.

I knew, in Toronto—it is long years ago—a singularly bright young man whose name was Robinson. He had had some training in the iron and steel business, and when I knew him was on the look out for an opening. I met him one day in a great hurry, with a valise in his hand.

"Where are you going?" I asked.

"Over to England," he said. "There is a firm in Liverpool that have advertised that they want an agent here, and I'm going over to apply for the job."

"Can't you do it by letter?" I asked.

"That's just it," said Robinson, with a chuckle, "all the other men will apply by letter. I'll go right over myself and get there as soon or sooner than the letters. I'll be the man on the spot, and I'll get the job."

He was quite right. He went over to Liverpool, and was back in a fortnight with English clothes and a big salary.

But I cannot recommend his story to my friends. In fact, it should not be told too freely. It is apt to be dangerous. I remember once telling this story of Robinson to a young man called Tomlinson who was out of a job. Tomlinson had a head two sizes too big, and a face like a bun. He had lost three jobs in a bank and two in a broker's office, but he knew his work, and on paper he looked a good man. I told him about Robinson, to encourage him, and the story made a great impression.

"Say, that was a great scheme, eh?" he kept repeating. He had no command of words, and always said the same thing over and over.

A few days later I met Tomlinson in the street with a valise in his hand. "Where are you going?" I asked.

"I'm off to Mexico," he answered. "They're advertising for a Canadian teller for a bank in Tuscapulco. I've sent my credentials down, and I'm going to follow them right up in person. In a thing like this, the personal element is everything."

So Tomlinson went down to Mexico and he traveled by sea to Mexico City, and then with a mule train to Tuscapulco. But the mails, with his credentials, went by land and got there two days ahead of him.

When Tomlinson got to Tuscapulco he went into the bank and he spoke to the junior manager and told him what he came for. "I'm awfully sorry," the junior manager said, "I'm afraid that this post has just been filled."

Then he went into an inner room to talk with the manager. "The tellership that you wanted a Canadian for," he asked, "didn't you say that you have a man already?"

"Yes," said the manager, "a brilliant young fellow from Toronto. His name is Tomlinson. I have his credentials here—a first-class man. I've wired him to come right along, at our expense, and we'll keep the job open for him ten days."

"There's a young man outside," said the junior, "who wants to apply for the job."

"Outside?" exclaimed the manager. "How did he get here?"

"Came in on the mule train this morning. Says he can do the work and wants the job."

"What's he like?" asked the manager.

The junior shook his head. "Pretty dusty looking customer," he said. "Shifty looking."

"Same old story," murmured the manager. "It's odd how these fellows drift down here, isn't it? Up to something crooked at home, I suppose. Understands the working of a bank, eh? I guess he understands it a little too well for my taste.

Tussapulco

No, no," he continued, tapping the papers that lay on the table, "now that we've got a first-class man like Tomlinson, let's hang on to him. We can easily wait ten days, and the cost of the journey is nothing to the bank as compared with getting a man of Tomlinson's stamp. And, by the way, you might telephone to the Chief of Police and get him to see to it that this loafer gets out of town straight off."

So the Chief of Police shut up Tomlinson in the calaboose and then sent him down to Mexico City under a guard. By the time the police were done with him he was dead broke, and it took him four months to get back to Toronto. When he got there, the place in Mexico had been filled long ago.

But I can imagine that some of my readers might suggest that I have hitherto been dealing only with success in a very limited way, and that more interest would lie in discussing how the really great fortunes are made. Everybody feels an instinctive interest in knowing how our great captains of industry, our financiers and railroad magnates made their money.

Here the explanation is really a very simple one. There is, in fact, only one way to amass a huge fortune in business management. One must begin at the bottom. One must mount the ladder from the lowest rung. But this lowest rung is everything. Any man who can stand upon it with his foot well poised, his head erect, his arms braced and his eye directed upward, will inevitably mount to the top.

But after all—I say this as a kind of afterthought in conclusion—why bother with success at all? I have observed that the successful people get very little real enjoyment out of life. In fact the contrary is true. On the way to becoming rich, they develop extreme caution with respect to preserving the wealth they have managed to accumulate, then forevermore think of nothing but that.

If I had to choose—with an eye to having a really pleasant life—between success and ruin, I should prefer ruin every time. I have several friends who are completely ruined—some two or three times—in a large way of course; and I find that if I want to get a really good dinner, where the champagne is just as it ought to be, and where hospitality is unhindered by mean thoughts of expense, I can get it best at the house of a ruined man.

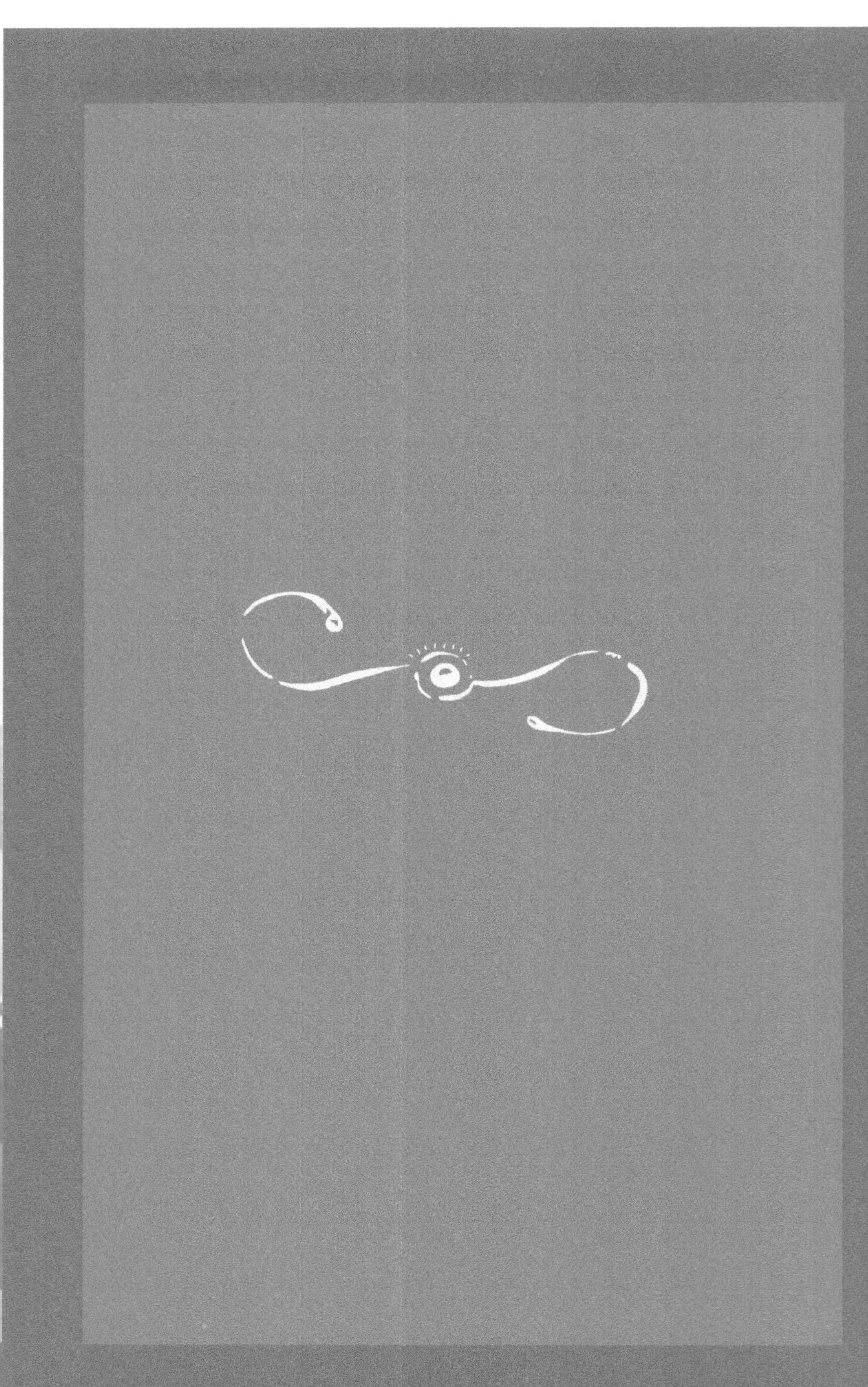

THIS STRENUOUS AGE

Something is happening, I regret to find, to the world in which we used to live. The poor old thing is being "speeded up." There is "efficiency" in the air. Offices open at eight o'clock. Millionaires lunch on a baked apple. Bankers eat practically nothing. A college president has declared that there are more foot pounds of energy in a glass of peptonized milk than in—something else, I forget what. All this is very fine. Yet somehow I feel out of it. My friends are failing me. They won't sit up after midnight. They have taken to sleeping out of doors, on porches and pergolas. Some, I understand, merely roost on plain wooden bars. They rise early. They take deep breathing. They bathe in ice water. They are no good. This change I am sure, is excellent. It is, I am certain, just as it ought to be. I am merely saying, quietly and humbly, that I am not in it. I am being left behind.

But turn to the broader and simpler question of work itself. In my time one hated it. It was viewed as the natural enemy of man. Now the world has fallen in love with it. My friends, I find, take their deep breathing and their porch sleeping because it makes them work better. They go for a week's vacation in Virginia not for its own sake, but because they say they can work better when they get back.

I know a man who wears very loose boots because he can work better in them and another who wears only soft shirts because he can work better in a soft shirt. There are plenty of men now who would wear dog-harness if they thought they could work more in it.

I know another man who walks away out into the country every Sunday—not that he likes the country—he wouldn't recognize a bumble bee if he saw it—but he claims that if he walks on Sunday his head is as clear as a bell for work on Monday. Against work itself, I say nothing. But I sometimes wonder if I stand alone in this thing. Am I the only person left who hates it?

Nor is work all. Take food. I admit, here and now, that the lunch I like best—I mean for an ordinary plain lunch, not a party—is a beef steak about one foot square and two inches thick. Can I work on it? No, I can't, but I can work in spite of it. That is as much as one used to ask, twenty-five years ago.

Yet now I find that all my friends boast ostentatiously about the meagre lunch they eat. One tells me that he finds a glass of milk and a prune is quite as much as he cares to take. Another says that a dry biscuit and a glass of water is all that his brain will stand. One lunches on the white of an egg. Another eats merely the yolk. I have only two friends left who can eat a whole egg at a time.

I understand that the fear of these men is that if they eat more than an egg or a biscuit they will feel heavy after lunch. Why they object to feeling heavy, I do not know. Personally, I enjoy it. I like nothing better than to sit round after a heavy lunch with half a dozen heavy friends, smoking heavy cigars. I am well aware that that is wicked. I merely confess the fact. I do not gloss over it.

Nor is food all, nor drink, nor work, nor open air. Along with these so-called physical efficiencies, there has spread abroad a perfect passion for information. Somehow if a man's stomach is empty and his head clear as a bell, and if he won't drink and won't smoke, he reaches out for information. He wants facts. He reads the newspapers all through instead of only reading the headings. He clamors for articles filled with statistics about illiteracy and alien immigration and the number of ships in the Chinese navy.

I know quite a lot of men who have actually bought the new Encyclopedia Britannica . What is more, they read the thing. They sit in their apartments at night with a glass of water at their elbow reading the encyclopedia. They say that it is literally filled with facts. Other men spend their time reading the Statistical Abstract of the United States (they say the figures in it are great) and the Acts of Congress, and the list of Presidents since Washington (or was it Ben Franklin?).

Spending their evenings thus, and topping it off with a cold baked apple, and sleeping out in the snow, they go to work in the morning, so they tell me, with a positive sense of exhilaration. I have no doubt that they do. But, for me, I confess that once and for all I am out of it. I am left behind.

Add to this all such rising dangers as taxing the rich, UFOs, safety belts, the rating of movies, voting rights for all regardless of gender, race, or religion, licenses to fish, hunt, drive, and marry—topped off by the duty of the citizen to take an intelligent interest in politics—and I admit that I shall not be sorry to go away from here.

But before I do go, I have one hope. I understand that down in Jamaica things are very different. Bull fights, dog fights, lots of pretty women. Plus street racing is openly permitted, without seat belts! Business never begins till eleven in the morning. Everybody sleeps after lunch, and clubs remain open all night. Marriage is allowed but rare. In fact, the general condition of morality, so they tell me, is lower in Jamaica than it has been anywhere since the time of Nero and the burning of Rome. Me for Jamaica. Leaving tomorrow.

THIS STRENUOUS AGE

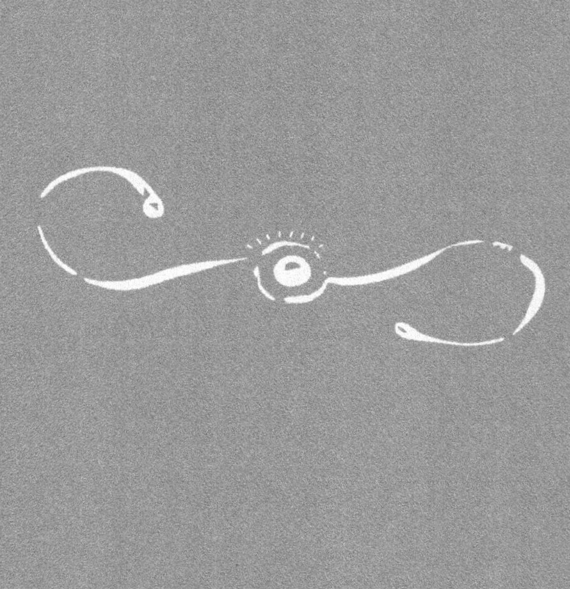

ARE THE RICH REALLY HAPPY?

ARE THE RICH REALLY HAPPY?

Let me admit at the outset that I write this essay without adequate material. I have never known, I have never seen, any rich people.

Very often I have thought that I had found them. But it turned out that it was not so. They were not rich at all. They were quite poor. They were hard up. They were pushed for money. They didn't know where to turn for ten thousand dollars.

In all the cases that I have examined this same error has crept in. I had often imagined, from the fact of people keeping fifteen servants, that they were rich. I had supposed that because a woman rode downtown in a limousine to buy a five-hundred-dollar hat, she must be well to do. Not at all. All these people turn out on examination to be not rich. They are cramped. They say it themselves. Pinched, I think, is the word they use. When I see a glittering group of eight people in a stage box at the opera, I know that they are all pinched. The fact that they ride home in a limousine has nothing to do with it.

A friend of mine who has ten thousand dollars a year told me the other day with a sigh that he found it quite impossible to keep up with the rich. On his income he couldn't do it. A family that I know who have twenty thousand a year have told me the same thing. They can't keep up with the rich. There is no use trying. A man that I respect very much who has an income of fifty thousand dollars a year from his law practice has told me with the greatest frankness that he finds it absolutely impossible to keep up with the rich. He says it is better to face the brutal fact of being poor. He says he can only give me a plain meal, what he calls a home dinner—it takes three men and two women to serve it—and he begs me to put up with it.

As far as I remember, I have never met Mr. Carnegie. But I know that if I did he would tell me that he found it quite impossible to keep up with Mr. Rockefeller. No doubt Mr. Rockefeller has the same feeling.

On the other hand there are, and there must be rich people, somewhere. I run across traces of them all the time. The janitor in the building where I work has told me that he has a rich cousin in England who is in the South-Western Railway and gets ten pounds a week. He says the railway wouldn't know what to do without him. In the same way the lady who washes at my house has a rich uncle. He lives in Winnipeg and owns his own house, clear, and has two girls at the high school.

But these are only reported cases of richness. I cannot vouch for them myself.

When I speak therefore of rich people and discuss whether they are happy, it is understood that I am merely drawing my conclusions from the people whom I see and know.

My judgment is that the rich undergo cruel trials and bitter tragedies of which the poor know nothing.

In the first place I find that the rich suffer perpetually from money troubles. The poor sit snugly at home while the Dow Jones Index falls a thousand points in a day. Do they care? Not a bit. An adverse balance of trade washes over the nation like a flood. Who have to mop it up? The rich. Call money rushes up to a hundred per cent, and the poor can still sit and laugh at a two-dollar moving picture show and forget it.

But the rich are troubled by money all the time. I know a man, for example—his name is Spugg—whose private bank account was overdrawn last month twenty thousand dollars. He told me so at dinner at his club, with apologies for feeling out of sorts. He said it was bothering him. He said he thought it rather unfair of his bank to have called his attention to it. I could sympathize, in a sort of way, with his feelings. My own account was overdrawn twenty cents at the time. I knew that if the bank began calling in overdrafts it might be my turn next. Spugg said he supposed he'd have to telephone his secretary 'in the morning to sell some bonds and cover it'. It seemed an awful thing to have to do. Poor people are never driven to this sort of thing. I have known cases of their having to sell a little furniture, perhaps, but imagine having to sell the very bonds out of one's desk. There's a bitterness about it that the poor man can never know.

With this same man, Mr. Spugg, I have often talked of the problem of wealth. He is a self-made man and he has told me again and again that the wealth he has accumulated is a mere burden to him. He says that he was much happier when he had only the plain, simple things of life. Often as I sit at dinner with him over a meal of nine courses, he tells me how much he would prefer a plain bit of boiled pork with a little mashed turnip. He says that if he had his way he would make his dinner out of a couple of sausages, fried with a bit of bread. I forgot what it is that stands in his way. I have seen Spugg put aside his glass of champagne—or his glass after he had drunk his champagne—with an expression of something like contempt.

He says that he remembers a running creek at the back of his father's farm where he used to lie at full length upon the grass and drink his fill. Champagne, he says, never tasted like that. I have suggested that he should lie on his stomach on the floor of the club and drink a saucerful of soda water. But he won't.

I know well that my friend Spugg would be glad to be rid of his wealth altogether, if such a thing were possible. Until I understood about these things, I always imagined that wealth could be given away. It appears that it cannot. It is a burden that one must carry.

Wealth, if one has enough of it, becomes a form of social service. One regards it as a means of doing good to the world, of helping to brighten the lives of others—in a word, a solemn trust. Spugg has often talked with me so long and so late on this topic—the duty of brightening the lives of others—that the waiter who held blue flames for his cigarettes fell asleep against a door post, and the chauffeur outside froze to the seat 'of his motor'.

Spugg's wealth, I say, he regards as a solemn trust. I have often asked him why he didn't give it, for example, to a college. But he tells me that 'unfortunately he is not a college man'.

I have called his attention to the need of further pensions for college professors—after all that Mr. Carnegie and others have done, there are still thousands and thousands of old professors of thirty-five and even forty, working away day after day and getting nothing but what they earn themselves, and with no provision beyond the age of eighty-five. But Mr. Spugg says that these men are the nation's heroes. Their work is its own reward.

But, after all, Mr. Spugg's troubles—for he is a single man with no ties—are in a sense selfish. It is perhaps in the homes, or more properly in the residences, of the rich that the great silent tragedies are being enacted every day—tragedies of which the fortunate poor know and can know nothing.

I saw such a case only a few nights ago at the house of the Ashcroft-Fowlers, where I was dining. As we went in to dinner, Mrs. Ashcroft-Fowler said in a quiet aside to her husband, "Has Meadows spoken?" He shook his head rather gloomily and answered, "No, he has said nothing yet." I saw them exchange a glance of quiet sympathy and mutual help, like people in trouble, who love one another.

They were my old friends and my heart beat for them. All through the dinner as Meadows—he was their butler—poured out the wine with each course, I could feel that some great trouble was impending over them.

ARE THE RICH REALLY HAPPY?

After Mrs. Ashcroft-Fowler had risen and left us, and we were alone over our port wine, I drew my chair near to Fowler's and I said, "My dear Fowler, I'm an old friend and you'll excuse me if I seem to be taking a liberty. But I can see that you and your wife are in trouble."

"Yes," he said very sadly and quietly, "we are."

"Excuse me," I said. "Tell me—for it makes a thing easier if one talks about it—is it anything about Meadows?"

"Yes," he said, "it is about Meadows."

There was silence for a moment, but I knew already what Fowler was going to say. I could feel it coming.

"Meadows," he said presently, constraining himself to speak with as little emotion as possible, "is leaving us."

"Poor old chap!" I said, taking his hand.

"It's hard, isn't it?" he said. "Franklin left last winter—no fault of ours; we did everything we could —and now Meadows."

There was almost a sob in his voice.

"He hasn't spoken definitely as yet," Fowler went on, "but we know there's hardly any chance of his staying."

"Does he give any reason?" I asked.

"Nothing specific," said Fowler. "It's just a sheer case of incompatibility. Meadows doesn't like us."

He put his hand over his face and was silent.

I left very quietly a little later, without going up to the drawing-room. A few days afterwards I heard 'that Meadows had gone'. The Ashcroft-Fowlers, I am told, are giving up in despair. They are going to take a little suite of ten rooms and four baths in the Grand Palaver Hotel, and rough it there for the winter.

Yet one must not draw a picture of the rich in colors altogether gloomy. There are cases among them of genuine, light-hearted happiness.

I have observed this is especially the case among those of the rich who have the good fortune to get ruined, absolutely and completely ruined. They may do this on the Stock Exchange or by banking or in a dozen other ways. The business side of getting ruined is not difficult.

Once the rich are ruined, they are, as far as my observation goes, all right. They can then have anything they want.

I saw this point illustrated again just recently. I was walking with a friend of mine and a motor passed bearing a neatly dressed young man, chatting gaily with a pretty woman. My friend raised his hat and gave it a jaunty and cheery swing in the air as if to wave goodwill and happiness.

"Poor old Edward Overjoy!" he said, as the motor moved out of sight.

"What's wrong with him?" I asked.

"Hadn't you heard?" said my friend. "He's ruined—absolutely cleaned out—not a cent left."

"Dear me!" I said. "That's awfully hard. I suppose he'll have to sell that beautiful motor?"

My friend shook his head.

"Oh, no," he said. "He'll hardly do that. I don't think his wife would care to sell that."

My friend was right. The Overjoys have not sold their motor. Neither have they sold their magnificent sandstone residence. They are too much attached to it, I believe, to sell it. Some people thought they would have given up their box at the opera. But it appears not. They are too musical to care to do that. Meantime it is a matter of general notoriety that the Overjoys are absolutely ruined— in fact, they haven't a single cent. You could buy Overjoy—so I am informed—for ten dollars.

But I observe that he still wears a seal-lined coat worth at least five hundred.

the end

STEPHEN LEACOCK (1869-1944)

At the age of seven, Stephen Leacock, a native Englishman, accompanied his parents to Ontario, Canada where they established residency and citizenship. Once in place as a Canuck, he proceeded to attain a rather wide-ranging education, culminating in master degrees in political science and economics and a doctorate in Philosophy. He went on to head the political science and economics departments at McGill University in Toronto, and it was there that he established a notable reputation as an academic economist. Given all this, many of his friends were under the impression that he wrote humorous essays in those idle moments when his wearied brain was unable to perform the serious labors of the economist. In fact, it was exactly the other way around. He found it no challenge to write instructive, academic treatises fortified by facts and figures. But to write something straight out of one's mind that was worth reading for its own sake was an arduous contrivance that he claims he only accomplished in few-and-far-between, fortunate moments.

Perhaps. And yet somehow between the years 1915 and 1925, he was the most popular humorist in the English speaking world. Leacock consistently forced belly laughter by poking fun at people's foolish acts and ideas and, as the collected essays in this volume show, excelled at adroitly balancing cutting satire with over-the-top absurdity. In these ways, he was rivaled only by Mark Twain, a humorist he greatly admired.

Just as worthy comedians and humorists in the USA are annually awarded the Mark Twain Prize for American Humor, worthy humor writers in Canada are annually awarded the Stephen Leacock Memorial Medal for Humour. This more than merely suggests Stephen Leacock made countless people in need of a hearty laugh grateful he found the time to arduously contrive award-winning humor that complemented his easy-peasy academic treatises.

The *Adapted Classics* Collection

Contemporary classic illustrations in *Adapted Classics* books add expression to visually-rich stories by world-famous authors. Lightly modified and illustrated to suit and attract modern young readers, stories in the *Adapted Classics* collection are respectful renditions of timeless stories from the world of classic literature.

View the entire collection at: www.adaptedclassics.com

Marc Johnson-Pencook is an illustrator, animator, and muralist. He lives in Minneapolis, Minnesota. His illustrations appear in books, periodicals, gallery shows and private collections, and his murals adorn many walls and ceilings in public places and private spaces in the Twin Cities and beyond. He also teaches illustration at the Atelier Studio Program of Fine Art in Minneapolis and the Art Academy in St. Paul. In addition, Marc composes and performs rock music—he currently plays percussion for Mod Gods of Nod—a psychedelic rock band based in Minneapolis. Marc can be contacted at: http://illustratormarc.com/

Jerome Tiller lives in Minneapolis, Minnesota. He is owner of ArtWrite Productions, a publishing company bent on making education and reading more pleasurable for youth. Adapted Classics, an imprint of ArtWrite Productions, uses fine-art illustrations to introduce classic stories to young readers. Learn more about Jerome and his company at: artwriteproductions.com and adaptedclassics.com

www.ingramcontent.com/pod-product-compliance
Lightning Source LLC
Chambersburg PA
CBHW040544170726
48295CB00012B/580